This igloo book belongs to

....

igloobooks

Published in 2019
by Igloo Books Ltd
Cottage Farm
Sywell
NN6 0BJ
www.igloobooks.com

Copyright © 2017 Igloo Books Ltd
Igloo Books is an imprint of Bonnier Books UK

1219 003
4 6 8 10 11 9 7 5
ISBN 978-1-78670-928-8

Written by Stephanie Moss and Melanie Joyce

Cover designed by Alice Dainty
Interiors designed by Amy Bradford
Edited by Hannah Campling

Printed and manufactured in China

Adventure Tales

igloobooks

I want to be a
Fireman

I want to be a fireman
and wear a **shiny** yellow hat.

I'd answer all **emergencies**
with my trusty fireman's cat.

When there's a **fire**, I'd get a call
and be **quick** as a flash.

When it rained, I'd race to **rescue** drivers that were **stuck**.

I'd pull them from the **squelchy** mud
with rope fixed to my truck.

I'd **jump** into my fire engine,
and we'd be on our way.

Fire Station

It really would be **fun**
to be a **fireman**, one day.

I want to be a Pirate

I'd **sail** my ship across high seas
into the **golden** sun.

I'd have a **parrot** as my pet
and a crew of twenty men.

I'd steer my ship to **mysterious** lands and **sail** it back again.

We'd find a **map** inside a **bottle**
and follow it to land.

It would show where the **treasure's** buried, underneath the sand.

My crew and I would search
for a **shining** treasure chest.

Then we'd head back to our ship
for the next **exciting** quest.

I want to be a Train Driver

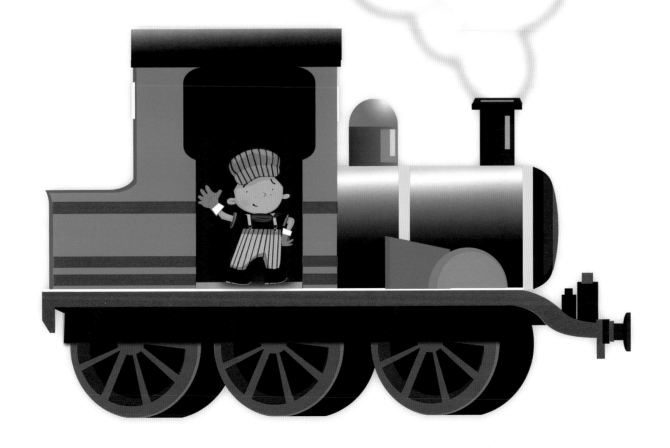

I want to be a **train** driver and **chug** along the track.

I'd take people on their **journeys**
and then I'd bring them back.

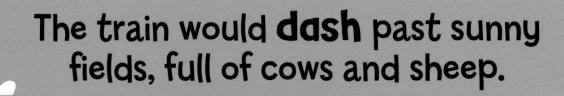

The train would **dash** past sunny fields, full of cows and sheep.

Children on the train would smile
to see the fluffy lambs **leap**.

When we arrived at the final station,
the **whistle** would go...

... WHOC
WHOO!

People would **hop** off the train,
wave goodbye and say, "**Thank you!**"